The Science of Passion,
the Art of Romance

KEN TANNER

Order this book online at www.trafford.com/-09-0505
or email orders@trafford.com

Most Trafford titles are also available at major online book retailers.

© Copyright 2009 Ken Tanner.

Artwork & cover design   Kim Smerek

Editing & layout   Davina Haisell,
                                Writer Sense Communications

Proofreading   Sharon McInnis,
                                ProofingQueen*

Note for Librarians: A cataloguing record for this book is available from Library and Archives Canada at www.collectionscanada.ca/amicus/index-e.html

Printed in Victoria, BC, Canada.

ISBN: 978-1-4269-1028-9 (Soft)
ISBN: 978-1-4269-1030-2 (ebook)

We at Trafford believe that it is the responsibility of us all, as both individuals and corporations, to make choices that are environmentally and socially sound. You, in turn, are supporting this responsible conduct each time you purchase a Trafford book, or make use of our publishing services. To find out how you are helping, please visit www.trafford.com/responsiblepublishing.html

Our mission is to efficiently provide the world's finest, most comprehensive book publishing service, enabling every author to experience success. To find out how to publish your book, your way, and have it available worldwide, visit us online at www.trafford.com/10510

 www.trafford.com

North America & international
toll-free: 1 888 232 4444 (USA & Canada)
phone: 250 383 6864 ♦ fax: 250 383 6804 ♦ email: info@trafford.com

The United Kingdom & Europe
phone: +44 (0)1865 487 395 ♦ local rate: 0845 230 9601
facsimile: +44 (0)1865 481 507 ♦ email: info.uk@trafford.com

10 9 8 7 6 5 4 3 2 1

"To my wife Carol, the
source of my romantic spirit.
Love you Darling."

————————————————

TABLE OF CONTENTS

PREFACE

There are many books available to help those with struggling marriages. This is <u>not</u> one of them. This book is directed at husbands in middle age (like me) who are in solid marriages, yet seek to make them stronger. Perhaps the spark has been missing – the many pressures of kids, work, associates and friends have sapped the energy. How can you reignite that spark, and redirect that renewed energy toward the one person who means so much in your life?

Fellows, that one person is your wife. She is the most important person to you, yet other priorities often overwhelm your relationship with her. You chide yourself for letting that happen, and you know in your heart that it is time to take control – time to redirect your energy toward sustaining and nurturing this most important relationship. It is time to focus the love that resides deep inside you, directly at her, reminding her that nothing is more important in your life than she is.

This book is for husbands with strong, stable marriages who want to rekindle the electric atmosphere. Rebuilding the "couple energy" you had in your early time together is not difficult to do – it's more a change of perspective and self-imagery than anything else.

Journey with me on a path toward imagining your marriage back into that passionate romantic relationship you know it can be.

INTRODUCTION

What makes a marriage work well? It seems strange that couples who share nearly identical economic, social and family circles often experience different outcomes in their marriages. Do you know of another couple with similar backgrounds and experiences who has a marriage that is perhaps much better, or maybe less successful than yours? What different ingredients might account for the disparity between a robust, productive marriage and one that struggles?

There! I've given away the first hint already. Love requires a recipe to be successful. Many ingredients are needed and all of them are essential. Imagine a cake made without sugar, or an omelette made with eggs that were not fresh. Although you have most of the necessary ingredients, some are missing or were not properly selected.

Love is like that. There are many ingredients. To have the perfect union, one needs to ensure that all the ingredients are both present and fresh. I call this the "Science of Passion" and it is exactly what this book talks about – the science of ensuring that all the ingredients of your marriage are present and fresh.

Ah, but the Art of Romance is where all the fun is. The Art is the individual's special contribution, the unique delivery of those ingredients in an event that is like no other. The Art is where your own personal signature resides, one your spouse recognizes as truly singular for her – meant only for her, delivered only by you.

Imagine two cakes that are identical, except one has your favourite picture of her digitally printed on the icing. Which cake do you think she will know came only from you? Same cake ingredients, but delivered in two very different ways.

Darn it. Now I've gone and given away the second secret. The "Art of Romance" is the *individualization of the message*. You present your event or gift in such a manner that she knows it could only have come from you. Your unique signature tells her that you put extra effort and thought into this, ensuring that she knows it was prepared just for her. The Art requires you to delve into your imagination so your event becomes a memorable moment – one she knows is hers alone.

So, let's start on our journey. This book explores 10 romantic scenarios, each focusing on the Science (the ingredients) and the Art (the unique presentation) of an event or gift. We'll focus on creating that perfect "cake", and on ensuring that your wife will know it was prepared especially for her. Science and Art together – that is what you are about to experience as never before.

CHAPTER ONE

Jewellery... from the display case or from your heart?

It's Friday evening after a tough day at work. Pressures have built all week. Time to get home. Halfway there you have a devastating thought – it is your anniversary weekend! Thank goodness the local jewellery store is open. You whip in. There's gotta be something there. The salesperson understands. Need something quick.

Two brooches look good – either one will do. Do they have a blank card that you can sign? One that says *you are special* in some weird scribbled font. Would never have written that, but it will have to do. Thank goodness they have wrapping paper at this jewellery store. It's kind of bland, but the ribbon looks nice – especially with that machine-made commercial bow that the salesperson applies with tape.

You know where this is going, don't you? Let's rewind the clock – back to a point perhaps three or four weeks earlier.

It's a Saturday afternoon and you have just noticed an ad in the paper about jewellery. A thought is triggered – "Our anniversary is in three weeks. Some jewellery would be a good idea this year." You take out a doodle pad and draw some lazy circles – hold it out and turn it sideways – kind of looks like a flower doesn't it? Draw in a petal or two, maybe a little leaf – straight stalk, no, scratch that – a curved stalk. Never was much of an artist. Oh well. Tuck it into your wallet. Let it simmer a bit.

At work on Monday you're having an awful day, but while you sit waiting for your meeting to start, you pull the paper out. Flower needs a few more petals. Perhaps it is a rose. It's nice to think of her once or twice during your day. The stalk needs to be a bit longer and it needs another leaf. Back into the wallet as the meeting finally gets started.

The jewellery store is conveniently located on your way home. Nice jeweller, and very proud of his work – he has been a jeweller for decades. Really innovative. You show him the sketch from your wallet. He takes it, pulls out another piece of paper, and more skilfully sketches your rose from another angle – adds some dimension to it. He suggests a way to add a pin so it won't show. Perhaps the outer petal could be shaped more like a heart? His wife is there. She comes out to see. The three of you spend 10 minutes mulling over the design. You leave him your business card.

The jeweller calls you at work on Tuesday afternoon. Offers to craft the design using a pliable metal covered with gold leaf. Not that expensive. He likes the idea and loves the challenge of an innovative design. He will have a wax model for you to look at on Friday after work. A five-minute stop on Friday confirms that the design looks great. You go home. The jeweller starts work on your design.

A week later, your personally designed brooch is ready. The jeweller's wife is impressed with you. She finds some nice wrapping paper and shows you how to tie a bow and spiral the ribbon. The love note that goes with it is in your own handwriting. You spent a half hour in the car on your way home planning what you wanted to say. Only 10 words, but they are all yours – and only for her.

The Science: A brooch. You know jewellery is always welcome – the acknowledged gift of your special love. The standard ingredient.

The Art: Here is where you shine! This design is unique, one-of-a-kind – never to be replicated. It is for her and her alone – from you and you alone. It's totally personal and intimately prepared for her. There is no other like it and no one else will ever have one. Your handwriting reflects the care you took. Your words are different than any of those sappy commercial notes, and mean so much more to her. She is overwhelmed, ecstatic even. She cries. She comes to you, reaches for you. You've connected once more as a special, unique couple.

So, what happened here? Time spent at the jeweller was perhaps 15 minutes. The original sketch took 10, writing your own note took 3, learning to spiral the ribbon took 30 seconds. This was not some gigantic time-consuming exercise in advanced artistic design.

All it really took was a little forward thinking, combined with a bit of imagination from deep within that Neanderthal male brain. The scrap of paper with the original sketch is amateurish, not sophisticated at all. But the delivery of the final product – well, that is sophistication at its finest – planned as an intimate moment, with a unique gift that came from you and you alone. That evening, more than a few sparks flew in your marriage – there were fireworks!

CHAPTER TWO

Dinner...
the restaurant's menu
or YOUR menu?

Hint: Now that you have read chapter one, can you guess how chapter two will end? The only difference is that there is more planning and preparation in chapter two. After all, you are now that much more connected with her, aren't you?

The reservation for Friday's dinner was easy. One phone call. Picked her up at home. No time to change because the reservation time was awkward. You are still in your office duds. Good thing there is a decent wine list, but they sure charge a lot for the good stuff. Appetizers, salad, soup, meal, dessert, cappuccino, and $200 later you are on your way home. Ho hum – all the way home. Ho hum at home too, I bet!

So, let's wind the clock back to the day before. You stopped in at the grocery store on the way home from work. Took a half hour to pick up the following:

1) A bag of lettuce with all sorts of different weeds mixed together. Croutons are right there next to the lettuce, as is a new salad dressing you've never tried.

2) A can of soup with a fancy name – a few steps above chicken noodle, say butternut squash. Sounds intriguing.

3) Steak is pricey tonight, but that pork tenderloin is reasonable and will cook on the BBQ really well. A bottle of meat spice to add some zing.

4) Potatoes are out – way too much preparation. But broccoli and a small bunch of carrots to add some colour would be good. Cheese sauce on the broccoli is a nice touch.

5) A large tomato and a bit of Parmesan cheese.

6) The bakery has two individual servings of crème brûlée – her sinful favourite.

7) A bottle of bubbly – mandatory.

8) A bouquet of flowers and two candles.

Friday evening arrives. She does not know what to expect as you have only told her to plan nothing for the evening. Since the evening is yours, there is no need to rush. No reservation time to meet.

A relaxed shower. Comfortable clothes. You prepare the evening adventure together. She sets the table with a fresh tablecloth, the good dishes and two champagne flutes. Candles are lit and flowers are in a small vase. She putters as she does this, singing gently to herself. She is relaxing and enjoying the anticipation of the surprise.

You have a tougher job. But the food choices were made in such a way that dinner is easy to prepare.

1) Lettuce tossed, croutons sprinkled on top, dressing in a small dish. First course done in three minutes.

2) Microwave the soup on medium for five minutes. Second course is complete.

3) Slice the tomato in half, sprinkle with Parmesan and grill for two minutes. Voila, third course.

4) Enjoy a few sips of bubbly while the pork sizzles on the BBQ. Microwave the broccoli and carrots together for three minutes on high. Warm the cheese sauce for one minute on high. Stir and drizzle over the broccoli. Main course ready.

5) Tell her you spent all afternoon preparing the crème brûlée from scratch – too bad about the office meeting. (I am sure she will believe you.)

Candles, flowers and champagne carry you both into the remainder of the evening. You reminisce and chat about those wonderful evenings you shared when you first met.

The Science: Dinner. Five courses. Straightforward. Not hard to prepare. Time to shop and cook totalled less than one hour.

The Art: Your meal, your selection, your menu – your personal signature on this particular evening.

CHAPTER THREE

The simple... can you make 50 balloons mean something?

It is easy to be impressed by someone, but difficult to figure out how to impress another person. One of life's little ironies.

Imagine the prelude to a special occasion. Perhaps 50 days before some significant event – anniversary, birthday, a trip you are planning together. She might never have thought that the 50th day before that lovely cruise you have planned might be a cause for celebration. Surprise her – with 50 "somethings" to celebrate that anticipated journey.

Could be balloons, flowers, chocolates, or her favourite treat – perhaps chocolate-covered strawberries? Let's use balloons as our example.

She is out for the afternoon. Go find 50 interesting balloons and a few weights at a local party store. Perhaps some red balloons shaped like hearts, or with the anticipated event written on them. Buy a few extra because some will pop. Inflate them with helium at the store, or use your lungs back at home. (I went with the helium – much easier. How you get them home from the store is your problem. I made two trips.) Ok, now you have 50 inflated helium balloons resting on the family room ceiling. Recipe complete.

The easy way out is to tie a string to them and hand them to her as she comes in the door. She will be amused and pleased that you are anticipating the upcoming cruise so much. "Now please go fix the broken handle on the front door."

So, the Art in this event needs to be the delivery. Overwhelm her so she forgets completely about that broken handle on the door. Fifty helium balloons on strings with weights will be the pathway to your special message. Start at the front door and place them sequentially, meandering through a few rooms. Three to five feet apart should do fine.

What red-blooded woman wouldn't follow a pathway of heart-shaped balloons? En route place a few teasers – waypoints with short messages taped to a few of the balloons. Here are some suggestions.

"Fourteen nights with only me." "Waves of love for both of us." "Candlelight dinners watching the moon sparkle on the ocean." "Champagne on our own ocean balcony." Whatever you wish.

At the end of the line, your message is loud and clear – "Happy 50 days till our cruise, darling. Can't wait to have you all to myself for 14 whole days! xoxoxoxo".

What was it that needed fixing again? I guess she can't think of it right now – too preoccupied with hugging and kissing you.

The Science: An unexpected celebration during the prelude to a special occasion or event. Celebrate the exact number of days leading up to this event with balloons or chocolates, or whatever else you choose.

The Art: Take her on a journey to reveal the surprise. Tease her along the way. Save the big message for the very end. You will just have to put up with the resulting hugs and kisses.

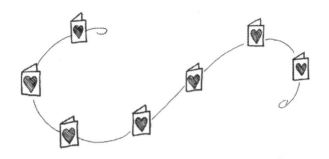

CHAPTER FOUR

A game of hide-and-seek...
notes that lead her only to you.

This is the simplest of all the ideas, and one of the most memorable. It is an adaptation of the balloon walk, except that there are no visible clues leading to each message. Hide-and-seek in its truest form.

It is your 15th anniversary. Go to the local stationery store and buy 15 small cards – perhaps the type that are used for invitations or place settings at a table.

Number each card as follows: 1 of 15, 2 of 15, 3 of 15, etc. Each card will share a special message. "You make my heart pound every time you enter the room." "I love the scent of your lavender perfume." "I love the small of your back." "I feel your loving presence whenever I come through the door."

Or, it may be a series of questions. "Do I think of you every day?" "Do I love to do things for you?" "Do I see you in every rose I find?" "Does your love bounce back – doubled?" Leave the last, most intimate message under her pillow. It will be the last one she finds on that particular evening.

The Science: Simple as can be – love notes for her. Fifteen different messages, one for each year of your marriage.

The Art: The search makes it fun. Each note triggers a giggle and a loving thought. The last one triggers whatever you want it to.

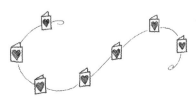

CHAPTER FIVE

Valentine's Day...
your moment to make or break.

Fear. Nervous trembling. Valentine's Day is two weeks away and you have no ideas. Things get worse. Now, Valentine's Day is upon you and still no ideas. Fear and trembling give way to terror and seizures. Amazing how sensitive skin can feel even more painful the closer you get to the fire!

Why are you letting yourself get so close to the fire? It will take no more effort to plan your event two weeks in advance than on the day of. The only difference is that two weeks in advance you have options, and on the day of the event you have very few.

Give yourself options. Stay back from the fire. Get to work on Valentine's Day in advance – it will take less effort than if you leave it to the last minute. Apply the two principles we are promoting in this book – Science and Art.

There are hundreds of gift ideas for Valentine's Day. Flowers, chocolates, clothes, lingerie, household implements... no, scratch that last one. I know someone who gave his new wife a sump pump. It did not go over well.

So, the recipe is firmly established. In your own experience I am sure there have been 10, 20 or 30 Valentine's Days. Trick question: How many do you remember? More importantly, how many does she remember?

The recipe is well-known, but the memory of the gift is eventually forgotten. The secret here is to create the memory as part of the gift. Science alone does not satisfy this requirement. Art is required to make it that memorable, unique experience – one that years later, she fondly keeps in her memory treasure chest.

Let me share a personal example. Once, I secretly left a dozen roses with my wife's hairdresser. He gave them to her after he finished washing her hair. Carol sat there through the entire cutting with the roses in her lap. Imagine the comments from the other patrons. Carol was queen for the day! Yes, there have been other bouquets of flowers during our 30 plus years of marriage, but she has never quite forgotten that unique delivery.

Now it's your turn. Here is a bit of homework. You are going to create your own answer to this chapter. Remember the last Valentine's Day gift you gave your lady? How could it have been delivered differently to make it more memorable?

Was there another location or time of day that would have had special meaning? Was there a different kind of wrapping paper or packaging you could have used, or a presentation that would have been more unique?

Maybe your gift could have been delivered anonymously, or while blindfolded (careful with that one!), or by someone unexpected. It could have been paired with something else – some food, drink, or a tasty treat. If you were going to do it again, how would you modify the delivery so that it would be truly memorable?

<u>Teacher here</u>: Your homework will be collected for marking in 10 minutes. The passing grade will be eventually determined by your wife.

CHAPTER SIX

Adorning the goddess... it's not the outfit that counts.

Beauty is in the eye of the beholder. This is a nice sentiment, but don't buy it. In your case, beauty is in the eye of the receiver!

I gave my wife the most memorable adornment she can recall. No cloth, leather or sequins. No rubber or poly. No silk or cotton. No sleeves, collars or cuffs. Memorable not for what it was, but for how I gave it to her.

I am referring to our 25th wedding anniversary cruise. (Note: the primary mission of the romantic is to foresee moments that have romantic potential well in advance of them occurring. Last-minute planning looks like last-minute planning.)

We had been planning this adventure for some time – a 10-day cruise through the Greek Islands. Lots to see every day. Romantic views of sandy beaches, crystal blue water and majestic buildings. Followed by more sandy beaches, crystal blue water, majestic buildings – you get the picture. But the opportunity to spend time together and share all of this every day made it a special and unique experience for both of us.

But I digress... back to the adornment. Before we left on our cruise, I spent more than a couple of afternoons exploring just about every lingerie outlet in town. My mission? To buy a different nightgown for her to wear on each night of our journey. I had a separately wrapped box for every night. Inside was a new nightie of various sorts (imagination required here). This was a total surprise to her on the first night. When I gave her the specially wrapped box on the second night, she figured out the game.

Every night she looked forward to her gift. The most memorable one I gave her was on the fifth night of our cruise. Instead of giving her a wrapped box, I asked her to remove her clothes and sit in front of the vanity mirror with her eyes closed. As I stood behind her with the gift hidden, I told her I was going to place that evening's nightwear on her. Adorning her neck with a gold chain and pendant, I fastened it and then gave her permission to open her eyes. I told her she was most beautiful clothed in such a special golden adornment. Tears, pleasure and happiness all followed.

<u>The Science</u>: Nightwear and a gold chain with pendant.

<u>The Art</u>: Specially chosen, beautifully wrapped nightwear, and a pendant gently placed around your loved one's neck – in a manner like no other.

CHAPTER SEVEN

The obvious... avoid it.
Be unique.

How many dozen roses do you think leave your local florist every day? No need to answer. Just realize it is a lot. How many are packaged in exactly the same way? Easy answer – almost all of them. So, although the flowers are nice, the true romantic will find a way to make the delivery unique and out of the ordinary – special for her.

I haven't bought a lot of flowers for Carol. Expensive things they are. It is only on a few special occasions that I splurge and buy a dozen of the finest reds. It was our 33rd anniversary. (Carol was mockingly furious that I called it our third-of-a-century anniversary, but that is another story.) Flowers were in order, but this time I wanted a unique delivery.

Imagination is required in these circumstances. Yours is likely as fertile as mine, so you will be able to adapt this idea to your own event. My idea? An oasis (that spongy green stuff they stick flowers in to hold them tightly) carved in the shape of a heart.

To symbolize our three decades together, I arranged the roses in three sections. I filled the upper portion with yellow roses, the middle with orange, and the bottom with red. White roses decorated the circumference. Dead simple to do – snip the roses short and construct your design. Voila, another unique delivery of a popular gift. Now, use your imagination!

<u>The Science</u>: Flowers for a special occasion and an oasis.

<u>The Art</u>: An arrangement that means something – a date, a place, a number. Get going!

CHAPTER EIGHT

Big effort, big rewards.

Now we take out the big guns. This is for one of those milestone events – likely a big anniversary. This one takes history, planning and effort, in that order. Get ready.

First, the history. The premise of this romantic gesture is to take her back to the earlier times the two of you spent together. You will reminisce and rekindle those memories with old photographs, favourite music, or by preparing meals that you both associate with those times. Any or all of these are important to help you trigger your memories. I bet you have lots of ideas of your own already!

This is the "away weekend" – Friday afternoon after work through to Sunday evening. It need not be physically away. In fact, it could be at your home or perhaps your cottage, but you are away mentally.

Basic arithmetic: Between Friday afternoon and Sunday evening there are seven meals – two breakfasts, two lunches and three dinners. There are likely seven special events that you have memories of, or perhaps seven places you have lived, or seven momentous moments that you have shared. Let's take the seven places you may have lived for this example.

There were most likely special foods associated with each of these locations. Perhaps dinners of salmon on the West Coast, or beef tenderloin from the Prairies. Do you remember Italian lunch hours from your days in New York, or seafood brunches from the Florida period? Breakfasts of crepes Suzette from Montreal, or those fabulous flapjacks with maple syrup from Vermont? Your choices can be elegant – lobster from Halifax, bluefin from Boston. Or, innovative – fajitas from California, tacos from Mexico.

Create a single meal from each of these locations – seven distinctive meals that reflect the period you lived there. The main course is best suited to be unique – bookend dinners with salad and a light dessert. If you have wine from that special period, pour it on. Breakfasts and lunches can each be a lighter, single course.

The meals will be memorable, but you can enhance them further with music from each period, and photographs from the family album. Then you will have a meal plan that can't be beat. Spend your mealtime reminiscing over photographs, dining on food that centred you in those places, and listening to background music from those eras. Candles? Mandatory. Hankies to wipe away happy tears? Optional.

Big effort? Absolutely! Planning, purchasing and preparing seven different meals is one heck of a task. But taking the time to cook them together, reminiscing over family photographs, talking about the times and people you met in each place – those are memories for a weekend getaway that will never be beat.

The Science: Seven meals, seven history markers, seven sets of photographs and memorable music.

The Art: Taking her through each of these periods is a joyous journey through your marriage. You both will re-awakenthe memories from your years together. A weekend walk down memory lane will warm her heart.

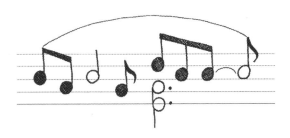

CHAPTER NINE

A love song? A painting?
A sculpture?

Does she like it when you hum a love song quietly as you go about your task? In the kitchen, helping with the dishes, you quietly hum a few bars of *And I Love Her.* (Perhaps the Beatles wouldn't recognize it, but she does.) She likes that touch – it brings the romantic out in you.

That is all well and good, but your chance to shine can go to a whole new level if you put your mind to it. Not all of us are musicians or lyricists, and we may never compete with Tony Bennett or Paul McCartney. But the musical Science and Art inside you can come through in a most elegant way if you put your mind to it. And for those who have other talents besides music – perhaps painting, poetry or sculpture – you can adapt to this model. Read on and modify these ideas to your specific hobby or talent.

A melody is easy to conceive. Hum a few bars and modify. Hum some more, modify and get it into your brain. Here's a tip for the musically challenged. Start with a tune you like, and modify it progressively with different notes. Record it on a mini-cassette recorder that can be purchased at an electronics store. Or buy some audio recording software from a computer store. Work on it gradually. Embellish, refresh and take a couple of weeks to make it sweet and soft. Compose a melody for both a verse and a chorus. First step complete.

Second step – lyrics to go with the melody. Single out an event (an anniversary would be a super choice). Write some simple lyrics to go with the tune you have composed. This does not have to be world-class – just coming from your heart will be classy in itself. There is a poet in you – bring him out of hiding.

One verse plus the chorus is a good start. Sentimental thoughts that are special to you both give a unique quality to your lyrics. At this point you might need help. You have a melody and a first draft. Ask a local piano teacher if there is a musician in the area who can transform your melody into a song. The musician will put accompaniment to the melody, flesh it out to give it depth and body. He will help with the lyrics, refining them to match the pace and tempo of the piece. You can be guaranteed that this musician will be into your love song. I am told that 90% of music is love songs.

Choices abound at this point – you can go as far as you are comfortable. The musician can record it to a CD and you will have your own special composition to give her. Or, you can sing and record it at his studio. A keepsake for all time.

The true romantics will take one extra step. They will have the musician record the music without the lyrics. Then, on the evening of that special anniversary, they'll light some candles in the living room, set her down with a glass of wine, put on the music CD, and sing her the song they have written. A quiet, intimate moment – truly unique and just for her.

I know, I know. This is a big one. And it may not be music that you choose. Perhaps you'll do a painting, write a poem or craft a sculpture – artistic help is nearby for these as well. Professional artists are just as easy to locate and engage as a professional musician. But true romantics know that a project like this can be worked on over a period of months.

The Science: Hum a melody, write it down or record it – verse and chorus. If you're a painter, pick up that paintbrush you have not touched for years. Bring your passion to the canvas.

<u>The Art</u>: Your words, your melody and your intimate delivery, all on a CD for her to treasure always. Or, perhaps your painting or sculpture – forever at her bedside.

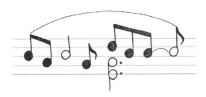

CHAPTER TEN

Surprise!
Put your best foot forward.

Military strategists emphasize the element of surprise. A successful campaign almost always involves the unexpected. The advantage the planner has is that he can influence the surprise so it has the greatest impact. Here is where you become the "Romantic Strategist". (How's that for a catchy title?)

What tools does the Romantic Strategist have in his toolkit? There are four of them. Unfamiliarity – finding something that is not familiar to her. Opportunity – finding an unexpected moment to spring the surprise. Scope – finding an event that is large, awe-inspiring and noble. Secretiveness – the fourth and most important tool. (It may be a secret from her, but not necessarily from those who are helping you plan the surprise.)

My example is dinner out. Dinners out are wonderful times to connect. Lingering by candlelight over a bottle of wine in an elegant hotel restaurant is wonderful. Too bad it has to end and you both have to climb into the car for the trek home. You're tired by that point, with a babysitter to pay and lunches to make for the next morning.

This is where the Romantic Strategist sees an opportunity. On the afternoon before dinner, you deliver her overnight bag to the concierge at the hotel where you plan to dine, and you check in at the front desk. Unbeknownst to her, you've packed her favourite nightie, a few of her important toiletries and a change of clothes.

Later, as dinner unfolds and with much effort, you keep your secret. A "big scope" moment is waiting for you both and she has no idea about your plans.

After dinner you take her hand and lead her to the elevator. Up to the 12th floor, and down the corridor. She is wondering just what you are up to as you unlock the door and lead her inside. The concierge has left the flowers on the table just as you requested, the chilled champagne is in the bucket, chocolates rest on both pillows and her overnight bag is sitting unopened at the foot of the bed.

The neighbour's wife (or grandma) has been in on your secret and generously agreed to watch the kids for the night. She stopped by your house and picked them up from the babysitter who was also in on the secret.

Your evening has just started. Time to relax in this special nest you have created. You talk into the night about each other, cuddle and relax in this most intimate setting. You have surprised her completely – even going so far as having a change of clothes waiting for her in the overnight bag at the foot of the bed. Good night. Sweet dreams.

<u>The Science</u>: Is booking a hotel room all that difficult? Deliver her nightie, clothes and things when you check in during the afternoon. Bring the babysitter, grandma or the neighbour's wife into the plan.

<u>The Art</u>: The Romantic Strategist pulls this off as a surprise. With everything taken care of, she has no need, nor want, that you have not already dealt with. Kids, clothes, dinner and an overnight adventure. Perhaps there is a surprise in store for you too!

AFTERWORD

Not an ending.
Just the beginning.

She wants your time and devoted attention more than anything else. It is the very best gift you can give.

Turn off your BlackBerry,® put away your iPod,® forget about your email and the bills – focus on her. No Internet, TV or computer. Set aside your personal organizer, the grocery list and the report that's due on Monday. They can wait. What can't wait is the expression of your devotion to her – that is all that matters.

Here is where we get confused. The "matrimonial home" has all sorts of assets – cars, kettles, irons, furniture, etc. The list is endless. The "matrimonial relationship" has fewer but more important assets – love, tenderness, passion, joy, intimacy and caring – but most of all, time. Time together is what she craves. Sure she is busy, as are you, but taking time to focus on her will be, without a doubt, the most important asset in your marriage.

The idea that your gift did not come from some online order catalogue, selected and purchased in five minutes, is critical to adding spark to your marriage. Your gift took ingenuity, insight, craftiness, inventiveness and, most of all, time to prepare. This is the most loving statement you can give her. It is a gift without words – a gift with feeling and passion. It is delivered in a unique way that is memorable and treasured.

Your marriage has survived many difficulties, as have all marriages. But yours is solid. Make it even more solid by giving her the one thing she craves most – your attention, your time, your passion for her and her alone. I promise – you will have a stronger marriage that sparkles with energy and vitality, and a wonderful life with the one you treasure the most.

MY OWN IDEAS

Printed in the United States